Who Is Gribich™

Story by **Marcus Porus**

Written by **Shirley Porus**

Illustrated by **Steven Jay Porus**

doog
PUBLISHING GROUP™

Library of Congress catalog card number: 95-92141
ISBN: 0-9646125-0-X

First Printing September 1995
10 9 8 7 6 5 4 3 2 1

[1. Childrens—Fiction 2. Space Travel—Fiction 3. Animals—Fiction]

This book is environmentally friendly.

Printed on recycled paper utilizing soy based inks.
Printed in the United States of America.

Contact Mac Art Direction for information or volume discounts.
7100 Sunnyslope Avenue, Van Nuys, CA 91405 818-764-6222

We dedicate this book to the child in all of us.

In memory of Dora Jaffe.
MP

In memory of Jacob Schneiderman.
SP

To Philip Lange who balances many lives.
SJP

One autumn day, deep in the forest, the animals were busy. They were fixing their homes and finding food for the winter.

Bobbin Robin was looking for grass and twigs to mend her nest. Cabot Rabbit was gathering dried grass to make her home warm and cozy.

Burl Squirrel was hiding food in an old tree trunk.

They never learned how to share or help each other. They only cared about themselves.

This made Cabot Rabbit angry.

"Give it back!" she demanded. "I saw it first," Bobbin said. "Did not!" said Cabot. Pretty soon they were having a big fight.

Suddenly, a beautiful, shiny, red ball appeared in the sky. It had flashing yellow lights all around it. The animals looked up, and there was a great hush throughout the forest.
What could this strange ball be, they wondered?
Could it be an airplane? No, it was too round.
Was it a bird? No, it didn't have wings.

The animals got scared. Bobbin forgot about her fight with Cabot and flew to the top of a tree.

Burl Squirrel ducked into a hole in a stump.

Cabot Rabbit didn't run away because she wanted to know what the strange ball was.

It floated slowly to the ground. The animals wondered what would happen next. Their hearts beat faster and faster!

Everyone
watched as
the ball opened.

A strange-looking
creature jumped
out.

He was like a colorful mushroom with arms and legs. He had large blue eyes and a big, friendly smile.

He said, "Hello o o o, hello o o o everyone."

The first one to answer the visitor was Cabot Rabbit. "Who are you? Why have you come to our forest? We don't like strangers here."

Burl Squirrel
popped his head
out of the tree
stump. He was
scared but curious.
He wanted
to have a
closer look.

"Where do you come
from?" he
asked.

Bobbin Robin flew to the ground. She wanted to hear every word.

The stranger said, "My name is Gribich. Don't worry, I won't hurt you. I come from the Planet Doog. I like to travel to other planets and make new friends.

But you don't look like you're friends. I saw you fighting when I was landing!"

Suddenly, a big wolf burst out of the trees.
HOWL L L L! He snarled fiercely and showed his
fangs. "I am Poof Wolf," he growled. The animals
backed away in fear.

"Why are you making so much noise?" Gribich asked.

In a gruff voice, Poof Wolf answered, "Because I am REALLY MEAN! You'd better be scared of me."

"I'm not frightened of anyone. Why are you so mean?" Gribich asked.

Poof stopped. His face got very sad. He said, "No one likes me. They won't talk to me. So why should I be nice to them?"

Gribich wanted to help them. But the animals would have to solve their problems for themselves. Gribich thought for a moment and said, "Long ago on the Planet Doog, no one would share. We cared only about ourselves. Because of this, we were lonely and unhappy.

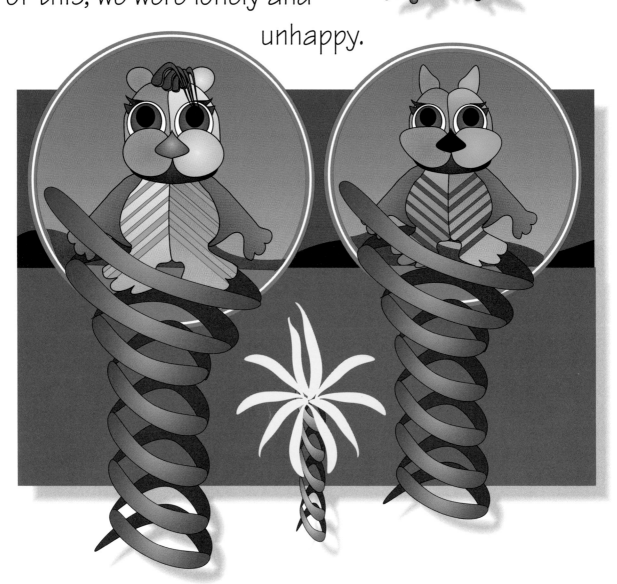

But slowly, we started trying to share
and be nice to one another.
After awhile, something
wonderful happened …
we became friends.
You can learn to
share, too.

You will be surprised
how much happier
you will be!"

The animals quietly listened to Gribich's story and thought about what he said. Bobbin Robin chirped, "Cabot, I am sorry I took your dried grass." Cabot Rabbit said, "I guess there's enough to share. You can have some too." Burl Squirrel said, "I want us to be friends. I have enough food stored for everyone.
I'll give you some."

Poof Wolf snorted, "And what about me?
All of you are so unfriendly to me.
It makes me mad!"

Cabot said, "I don't want to be friends when you growl so loudly."

Burl said, "You always snarl and show your fangs."

Bobbin said, "You scare us."

Poof Wolf answered quietly, "I am sorry. I was snarling because I was angry and lonely. If I stop doing that, can we be friends?"

Bobbin, Cabot and Burl talked among themselves. Together they said, "Yes, we will be your friends."

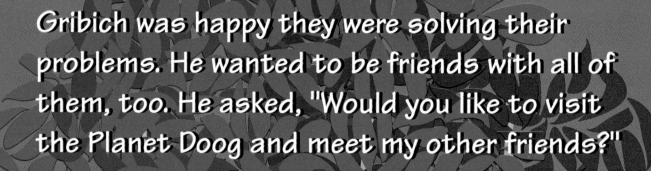

Gribich was happy they were solving their problems. He wanted to be friends with all of them, too. He asked, "Would you like to visit the Planet Doog and meet my other friends?"

Burl, Cabot and
Bobbin answered,
"Yes! we would love to go with you."

But Poof
Wolf was
sad. "I can't go with you because I am too big,"
he said. Gribich smiled and said, "Of course you
can. Next time I visit, I will bring a spaceship big
enough for all of us." Everyone was excited.

But it was getting late and it was time for Gribich to leave. All of the animals followed him to his space ship. They waved goodbye as Gribich climbed in. He was happy because he found new friends.

"Goodbye, I'll see you soon!" Gribich called. He waved to them all as the hatch closed.

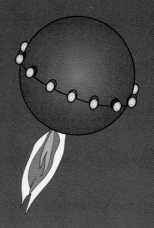

Then, just as suddenly as it had appeared,
the space ship vanished.

The End. . . Or is it?

We would like to acknowledge
Shannon Hickey
for her editorial direction.

We would also like to thank
Elena A Escalera, MA
Jose A. Feito, MA
Melanie Sandberg
Shoshana Phoenixx
for their editorial contributions.